17299

796.94
PAY
C.2
#25.00

S0-ACC-907

OUTDOOR LIFE

essential

SNOWMOBILING

for teens

Gregory Payan

Children's Press
A Division of Grolier Publishing
New York / London / Hong Kong / Sydney
Danbury, Connecticut

To Dee, taken before her time.

Book Design: Lisa Quattlebaum
Contributing Editor: Jennifer Ceaser

Photo Credits: pp. 5, 26 © Jamie Squire/Allsport; p. 6 © Carl Eliason & Company, Inc.; p. 10 © AFP/Corbis; p. 12 © Chaco Mohler/Mountain Stock; p. 15 © Kevin Woodward/Mountain Stock; p. 17 © Kevin Syms/Mountain Stock; pp. 18, 24 (1, 4) © Superstock; pp. 21, 24 (2), 28 © Hank deVré/Mountain Stock, p. 24 © Tim Bottomley/Mountain Stock; p. 36 © Dean Siracusa/FPG; p. 39 © Mike Powell/Allsport.

Visit Children's Press on the Internet at:
http://publishing.grolier.com

Library of Congress Cataloging-in-Publication Data

Payan, Gregory.
    Essential snowmobiling for teens / by Gregory Payan.
        p. cm.—(Outdoor life)
    Includes bibliographical references and index.
    ISBN 0-516-23358-0 (lib. bdg.)—ISBN 0-516-23558-3 (pbk.)
    1. Snowmobiling I. Title. II. Outdoor life (Franklin Watts, Inc.)

GV856.5 .P29 2000
796.94—dc21

                                                    99-055437

CONTENTS

Introduction

One cold December morning, you wake up to 12 inches (30 cm) of freshly fallen snow. Chances are, you won't be able to walk very easily in all that snow. Fortunately, you have your snowmobile ready to hit the trails. After a quick breakfast and a safety check, you're ready to go. Minutes later, you're cruising through the woods at 50 miles (80 km) per hour on trails that are in better shape than are most roads.

Snowmobiling is a sport that offers speed and excitement. It also allows people to go places they never dreamed possible—over snow, ice, and rugged mountain trails. All you need to have a great time snowmobiling is a sense of adventure, a love of the outdoors, and some warm clothing.

Snowmobiling is an exciting winter sport.

1
History of the
Snowmobile

Carl J. Eliason with one of his first snowmobile
designs, around 1926

Most people consider Carl J. Eliason to be the inventor of the first snowmobile. Eliason lived in Wisconsin, where it was often very difficult to travel because of heavy snowfall. Eliason also suffered from foot trouble, which made it hard for him to get around even in good weather. These difficulties inspired Eliason to create a machine that would travel over snow quickly and safely.

For two years, from 1922 to 1924, Eliason worked on building such a machine. His first version of the snowmobile was produced in 1924. It was a wooden toboggan (a long, flat-bottomed sled) with the back cut out. Eliason attached a track system with wooden cleats (similar to the treads on bulldozers). These cleats gripped the snow as the sled moved. A small, gas-powered engine turned the tracks. The front of the sled had two wooden skis.

Ropes were used to steer the vehicle. Eliason's invention was a success, and he received a patent for it in 1927.

The earliest versions of Eliason's snowmobile only went about 5 miles (8 km) per hour. By 1932, Eliason had improved the technology. His snowmobiles could reach speeds of up to 40 miles (64 km) per hour. By comparison, today's snowmobiles can go as fast as 120 miles (193 km) per hour!

SNOWMOBILE DEVELOPMENT

At about the same time that Eliason was building the first snowmobile in the United States, Canadian Joseph-Armand Bombardier was working on his version. On New Year's Eve 1922, when he was just fifteen years old, Bombardier revealed his invention. He had attached a car engine and a wooden propeller to a sleigh. The engine turned the propeller, and the propeller used air to push the sleigh.

Bombardier's brother sat at the front of the sleigh and steered it with his feet. The brothers drove the vehicle for almost a kilometer (about half a mile) through the streets of Valcourt, Quebec.

Snowmobiling Tip

Snowmobilers even have a museum dedicated to their sport. The New Hampshire Snowmobile Museum has about eighty vehicles—from the earliest to the most modern.

By 1936, Bombardier had created a snowmobile that could carry seven people at a time. One year later, he received a government patent for this model. Bombardier's company soon began producing two hundred snowmobiles a year. Doctors, priests, veterinarians, and wealthy people bought these early versions of the snowmobile. Later models carried as many as twenty-five children to school during the winter. In 1958, Bombardier decided to build a smaller, lighter

One of Bombardier's first snowmobile designs

snowmobile that the average person could afford. By 1959, he and his son had invented the Ski-Dog. It was later renamed the Ski-Doo. The Ski-Doo was the first snowmobile built just for recreation. It was made to be ridden by one or two people. Bombardier's Ski-Doo serves as the model for most of today's snowmobiles.

ON THE RISE
In the 1960s and '70s, snowmobiling became very popular. By 1974, about 500,000 snow-mobiles were being sold each year. Today,

there are more than four million snowmobiles in North America. Arctic Cat, Polaris, Ski-Doo, and Yamaha are the four major manufacturers of snowmobiles. Each year, these companies produce more than 250,000 snowmobiles in dozens of different models. These new machines are much better than the older models. Snowmobiles made in the 1960s and '70s were noisy, slow, and very undependable. At one time, snowmobilers spent an average of one hour fixing their machines for every two hours that they spent riding them.

In the 1990s, snowmobile manufacturers began making improvements. They built larger machines for a steadier and more comfortable ride. They used lighter materials so the machines could go faster. In comparison with older models, today's snowmobiles are cleaner, quieter, and easier to steer. They also feature heated handgrips and high, curved windshields for protection against the wind.

2
How to Participate

In most places, you must have a driver's license to operate a snowmobile.

So, just what does it take to be a part of the snowmobiling craze? Usually, the only thing you'll need to operate a snowmobile is a driver's license. Even if you don't have a license, you still may be able to drive a snowmobile in some parts of the United States and Canada. Each state or Canadian province has certain requirements for riders. In many places, teens who are under the driving age can take a safety course and earn an operator's permit. Young people also can participate by riding along with a parent or guardian.

THE COST

The United States and Canada require riders to have trail permits and to register their snowmobiles. These documents are not very expensive. However, snowmobiles are not cheap. Most new vehicles sell for about U.S. $6,000. But there are ways for you to get out on the trails.

Many companies throughout North America organize snowmobile tours during the winter. These tours can be for as short as two hours or as long as two weeks. Tours are designed for beginning, intermediate, and experienced riders. The cost of a tour that includes a guide ranges from U.S. $49 to $300. This includes the rental of a snowmobile and of snowmobile clothing. Day trips usually cover 30 to 75 miles (48 to 120 km) of trails. Overnight trips require snowmobilers to ride distances of 100 to 150 miles (160 to 240 km) each day. On a tour, you'll get to experience the beauty of the outdoors and also meet interesting people from all over the world. If you don't want to go on a tour, there are many areas where you can rent a snowmobile and snowmobile gear for as little as U.S. $85 per day.

WHERE TO SNOWMOBILE

There are 230,000 miles (370,300 km) of marked trails throughout the United States and Canada. Wisconsin has the most, with more than 25,000 miles (40,000 km) of trails. These trails wind through different towns, states, and provinces. They also lead to favorite winter vacation spots, hotels, and festivals. Top U.S. sites include Jackson Hole, Wyoming, the Colorado Rockies, Yellowstone National Park, and the upper part of Michigan. Ontario and Quebec have some of the best trails in Canada. Quebec also is home to the Valcourt International Snowmobile Festival, which is held every February.

Twenty-seven U.S. associations, twelve Canadian associations, and three thousand snowmobile clubs in North America work together to design and maintain the trails. These associations and clubs keep the trails

Snowmobiling in Idaho

safe. They work to train people to be safe snowmobilers, too. Local snowmobile clubs and associations help during emergencies. They are familiar with trails in their area and can assist with search-and-rescue operations for people who may be lost or injured. Snowmobile clubs also raise millions of dollars each year for charity.

3
Getting Started

It's important to dress warmly for snowmobiling.

One of the most important things to think about before driving a snowmobile is the kind of clothing you need to wear. Wear layers of clothing, so that you can add or remove layers as the weather changes. New types of fabrics, such as Gore-tex, allow snowmobile clothing to be windproof, lightweight, and stylish. Snowmobilers always should wear thermal underlayers, especially those made of silk. You also should look for clothing made of polyprolene. Polyprolene is a manmade material that is waterproof. All these fabrics help to keep your body warm when you are in cold, wet, and windy weather.

Avoid clothing made of cotton, such as sweatshirts, because cotton holds moisture. The goal of wearing protective clothing is to avoid hypothermia, which is extremely dangerous.

Snowmobiling Tip

To avoid sunburn, be sure to wear a high SPF sunscreen at all times. Snow acts as a reflector, making the sun even more intense than it can be in summer!

Hypothermia occurs when your body is exposed to wind, wetness, and cold temperatures. During hypothermia, the body loses heat faster than the heat can be replaced. The temperature of the body begins to drop. A person shivers, loses concentration, and breathes more slowly. If you experience any of these symptoms, leave the trail immediately and go to someplace warm.

You'll need to protect your face and head by wearing a helmet. Sunglasses or goggles will protect your eyes from the sun. When riding at night, attach reflectors to your clothes so that other drivers can see you.

A helmet and goggles need to be worn when riding on a snowmobile.

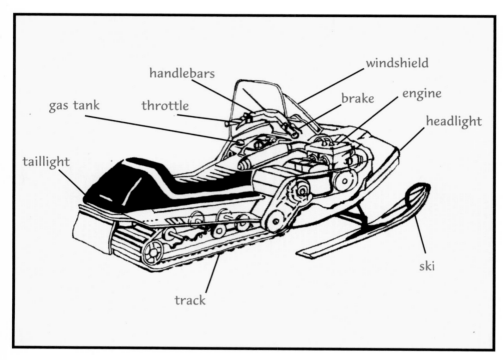

Parts of a Snowmobile

ABOUT YOUR SNOWMOBILE

Now that you're dressed to ride, it's time to get to know your snowmobile. Most snowmobiles weigh about 500 pounds (225 kg). They can carry up to two people. Some snowmobiles, such as racing models, weigh less and are made for just one person. Handlebars are attached to skis in the front of the vehicle and are used for steering. The brake stops the machine. The throttle controls the speed. The tracks and suspension system in the back of the snowmobile absorb bumps as you ride. The gas tank holds about 10 gallons (38 liters). You can travel for about 120 miles (193 km) before you need to get more gas. Today's engines can go as fast as 120 miles (193 km) per hour.

Riding a snowmobile is similar to riding a bicycle or motorcycle. Your body movements help you to steer and control the vehicle. Shifting your body weight and changing positions helps you to keep your balance. Knowing these positions will help you to react quickly to different snow and weather conditions, as well as changes in the terrain.

DRIVING POSITIONS

 **Sitting.** This is the most common and the safest position. It keeps your weight low and makes it easy to shift and steer.

 **Kneeling.** This position is helpful when leaning into a hill or steep slope. It also allows you to see over a rise in the trail. Maintain a slow speed in this position.

 **Standing.** This should only be done at slow speeds when trying to see more clearly what is ahead. Bend your knees slightly to absorb any bumps.

 **Posting.** A crouched position that is used only when riding over rough terrain. Posting allows the legs to absorb the shock of large bumps.

Driving Tips

- Before starting the engine, be sure the snow-mobile is not in reverse gear.
- Sit so that your weight is on the back of the vehicle. If you are sitting too far forward, it will be difficult to steer. Grip the handlebars firmly to keep control while steering.
- Begin by driving slowly for a short while to warm up the engine. To conserve energy and reduce gas fumes, don't run the engine unless you are driving it.
- Maintain your speed while going uphill. You will need to apply more gas to get up the hill, especially if the snow is deep. As you climb, lean forward in a standing or kneeling position. Do not stop as you are going uphill. You run the risk of getting stuck or sliding back down the hill.
- As you approach a curve, lean in the same direction you are turning. Be ready to shift your weight quickly when approaching bumps

Lean into a curve in the same direction you're turning.

and dips in the trail. When there are two riders, both the driver and the passenger should lean or shift their weight in the same direction.

• Reduce your speed as you go over the top of the hill and begin heading down. If you go downhill too quickly, you can lose control of the vehicle. Remain in a sitting position when descending.

Maintenance

Before you take the snowmobile out for a drive, there are five things that you should check. Use the word FELTS to help you remember:

F Fuel and oil levels—are the tanks full?

E Emergency stop switch—is it in the "up" position?

L Lights—are the headlights and taillights working?

T Throttle and brakes—press and release to be sure that they move and are not frozen.

S Steering—should move easily.

Always pack an emergency survival kit, no matter how short the trip. This should include a blanket, compass, first-aid kit, knife, matches, mirror, snacks, and extra clothing. Anything can happen in the wilderness, so it's important to be prepared.

4
Driving Safely

Unsafe driving results in thousands of snowmobiling accidents each year.

Each winter season, about ten million people in North America look forward to snowmobiling. Unfortunately, many drivers do not pay attention to safety issues. Unsafe driving results in thousands of snowmobiling accidents and hundreds of injuries and deaths each year. These involve not only snowmobile riders but also other people who are on or near the trails. During a recent fourteen-month period in New Hampshire, there were 165 injuries and twelve deaths from snowmobiling accidents. In Alaska, between 1993 and 1994, there were more injuries and deaths resulting from snowmobiles than from on-road vehicles.

Alcohol, speeding, off-trail riding, and thin ice cause most snowmobiling accidents and deaths. Also, most accidents occur at night, when it's more difficult to see possible dangers. Additionally, 80 percent of drivers involved in fatal accidents did not have a snowmobile safety certificate.

Alcohol

As with driving a car, operating a snowmobile after drinking alcohol is the quickest way to cause an accident. Alcohol is involved in nearly 70 percent of all fatal snowmobile accidents. Alcohol reduces a person's ability to react to other vehicles or dangerous obstacles. Drinking alcohol also increases your chances of contracting hypothermia. Alcohol tricks your body into thinking that it's warmer than it really is. In most areas, it is a crime to operate a snowmobile under the influence of alcohol.

Speed

Always ride at a comfortable speed. You should be able to see any obstacle within your sightline. Move at a speed at which you can avoid an obstacle or stop your vehicle quickly, if necessary. Slow down at night or in bad weather, when it's more difficult to see possible dangers. Also reduce your speed when you approach the top of a hill, road crossings, other vehicles, or people. You also should slow down when you see trees, animals, boulders, bodies of water, or other large objects.

Snowmobiling Tip

Show respect for wildlife. Animals, especially large ones, often use trails for walking. Stay at a safe distance and they will eventually move off the trail.

Off-Trail Riding

Even though 80 percent of snowmobiling is done on trails, nearly 80 percent of all snowmobiling accidents occur when people drive off the trails. Off-trail riding is illegal in most places. When a snowmobiler rides off the trails, he or she must be much more aware of

Snowmobiling and the Environment

Many people fear that snowmobiles have a negative effect on wildlife and the environment. However, studies have shown that snowmobiles, when driven safely on maintained trails, do not harm wildlife or the environment. Studies have proven the following:

- Snowmobiles do not drive away animals. Animals will only run away in fear when a snowmobiler gets off his vehicle and approaches them on foot.
- A snowmobile's weight is evenly distributed. This means that the pressure a snowmobile puts on the ground is less than that of a hiker.
- By law, snowmobiles are not allowed to produce more than 73 decibels of sound at a distance of 50 feet (14 meters). This is less noise than a vacuum cleaner makes.
- Manufacturers have greatly reduced the amount of exhaust, or fumes, that snowmobiles release into the air.

possible dangers. Unlike trails, wilderness areas have not been maintained. This means that hazards, such as rocks, fences, tree stumps, and branches, are more likely to be present.

Thin Ice
Many snowmobiler fatalities occur when the vehicle falls through ice. Before you drive over ice, you should know how thick it is. Check with your local trail organization before you start your ride. They can tell you the thickness of the ice on a particular body of water. The ice should be at least 5 inches (12 cm) thick before you travel across it. Many states also recommend that you wear a snowsuit equipped with a flotation device.

Night Riding
Snowmobiling at night is permitted, but there are certain rules that you should follow. Since

nine out of ten snowmobiling fatalities occur after dark, these rules are very important. Slow down and make sure not to overdrive your headlight. Overdriving means going so fast that the headlight is not lighting the road at a safe distance in front of you. Ask yourself, "Am I driving slowly enough to see an object in time to avoid hitting it?" Also, always wear reflective decals on your arms, back, and helmet when riding at night.

RESPONSIBLE RIDING

It's a good idea to buy a map and become familiar with the area where you plan to snowmobile. Whenever possible, ride with a friend or a group. It's safer and always more fun. If you will be riding alone, make a snow plan so that others will know where you are going and when you plan to arrive. Stay on marked trails. Follow all of the rules for snowmobiling in the state or province in which you are riding. Most important, always take a safety course! Snowmobile clubs and associations offer safety instruction and safety certification programs.

In addition to the safety measures already discussed, always use approved snowmobile hand signals (shown below).

Left turn	Right turn	Stop	Slowing

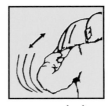

Sleds coming	Sleds behind	Last sled
Motion with arm three times over head.	Extend thumb. Motion three times toward sleds behind.	Motion from handlebar to ground three times.

5
The Future of the Sport

Racing snowmobiles are equipped with
powerful engines.

More than ever, young people are getting involved in snowmobiling. In 1998, nearly 10 percent of snowmobilers were under twenty-five years of age. Women's participation also is increasing. In fact, women purchase one out of every three new snowmobiles.

Many new snowmobiling competitions and racing events also have been established. Racing snowmobiles are specially designed and equipped with powerful engines. Snowmobiles compete in endurance races, where teams drive over long distances; drag races; and two of the newest events—hillclimbing and snocross.

HILLCLIMBING

A hillclimbing competition seems fairly simple at first glance. Riders point their vehicles straight up a slope and race to the top. The first person to make it to the top of the hill wins. There's more to it than just speed, though. A hillclimbing course can be 4,000 feet (1,213 m) long and 1,500 feet (455 m) in height, with jumps and gates throughout. This means that when a racer loses control during a jump, which happens quite often, the vehicle may begin to roll wildly down the slope. To avoid injury to other riders, there are people on hand to lasso the runaway vehicle.

SNOCROSS

Snocross is one of the newest games for people who like extreme sports. Snocross's recent appearance in the ESPN Winter X-Games made it a big hit, especially among young people. Snocross competitions take place on a half-mile course. The course includes bumps, jumps, and sharp, banked turns. Drivers approach speeds of 75 miles (120 km) per hour while flying 25 feet (8 m) in the air and jumping 100 feet (30 m) forward over the biggest jumps.

In snocross competitions, drivers reach very high speeds and fly in the air over big jumps.

Racing may not be for you (at least not yet), but you can still take part in the excitement of snowmobiling. In fact, 94 percent of snowmobilers consider it a family sport. Encourage your family to participate. Your parents may even want to go on a tour as part of your next family vacation.

SAFETY TIPS

The ISMA Snowmobiler's Pledge:

- I will never drink and then drive a snow-mobile.

- I will drive within the limits of my machine and my own abilities.

- I will obey the rules and laws of the state or province I am visiting.

- I will be careful when crossing roads, and always will cross at a right angle to traffic.

- I will wear appropriate clothing, including gloves, boots, and a helmet with a visor.

- I will let family or friends know my planned route, my destination, and my expected arrival time.

- I will treat the outdoors with respect. I will not litter or damage trees or other vegetation.

- I will respect other people's property and rights and will lend a hand when I see someone in need.

- I will not snowmobile where it is prohibited.

Practice Makes a Better Rider:

- Practice at slow speeds.

- Practice doing figure 8s in a flat area.

- Practice going uphill and downhill.

- Practice stopping at different speeds and under different weather and terrain conditions.

- Practice making hand signals.

- Practice leaning into turns.

NEW WORDS

banked tilted sideways

cleat something that sticks out from an object to prevent slipping

decal something designed to be attached to clothing, metal, or other material

drag race a short race to determine which vehicle can go the fastest from a standstill

exhaust gas fumes

flotation having the ability to float

hillclimbing a snowmobiling event in which vehicles race to the top of a hill

hypothermia a dangerous condition in which one's body temperature is well below normal

kilometer metric unit that equals about half a mile

maintenance upkeep and care of something

overdrive driving at such a high speed that the headlight can no longer provide enough light ahead of the vehicle

patent document that gives someone the right to produce and sell an invention

permit a certificate given to someone who is qualified to do a particular thing

polyprolene a manmade waterproof material

posting a crouched position

propeller a turning device that moves a vehicle, such as a plane, using air power

province a territory in a country, similar to a state

reflector something that reflects light

snocross an extreme sport where snowmobiles race on a course filled with jumps, bumps, and steep turns

suspension system a system of springs, shock absorbers, and other parts that give the vehicle a smooth ride

terrain the surface features of an area of land

thermal something designed to keep in heat

throttle part of a vehicle that changes its speed by supplying more or less fuel to the engine

toboggan a long, wooden, flat-bottomed sled

RESOURCES

(ISMA) International Snowmobile Manufacturers Association
1640 Haslett Road, Suite 170
Haslett, MI 48840
Tel: (517) 339-7788
Web site: *www.snowmobile.org*
ISMA provides statistics, history, safety tips, and links to other snowmobiling sites. Gives snowmobiling information upon request.

Ontario Federation of Snowmobile Clubs
12-106 Saunders Road
Barrie, ON
L4N 9A8
Tel: (705) 739-7669
Web site: *www.ofsc.on.ca*
Provides club and trail information for the Ontario, Canada, area. Includes general safety tips and registration and permit

information. Provides links to local snowmobiling chapters.

The Snowmobiling Network
www.snowmobiling.net
Provides links to international snowmobiling
areas, clubs, and associations. Has general
information about snowmobiling and more
detailed links to area trail conditions.

FOR FURTHER READING

Books

Hallam, Dave and James Hallam. *Snowmobiling: The Sledder's Complete Handbook*. British Columbia: Fun on Snow Publications, 1999.

Mara, W.P. *Snowmobile Racing*. Mankato, MN: Capstone Press, 1999.

Magazines

American Snowmobiler
P.O. Box 253
Newport, MN 55055
Subscriptions: (800) 935-2537
Web site: *www.amsnow.com*

SnoWest
520 Park Avenue
Idaho Falls, ID 83402
Subscriptions: (800) 657-5577
Web site: *www.snowest.com*

Index

About the Author

Gregory Payan is a freelance writer living in Queens, NY.